Alexander d. C. Scott

A Review of the Economic Position and Liabilities of the

Argentine Republic

Alexander d. C. Scott

A Review of the Economic Position and Liabilities of the Argentine Republic

ISBN/EAN: 9783337378172

Printed in Europe, USA, Canada, Australia, Japan

Cover: Foto ©Andreas Hilbeck / pixelio.de

More available books at **www.hansebooks.com**

A Review

OF THE

ECONOMIC POSITION AND LIABILITIES

OF THE

Argentine Republic.

BY

MAJ.-GENERAL A. DE C. SCOTT

(Late Royal Engineers).

" Nothing extenuate,
Nor set down aught in malice."—
OTHELLO, Act v., Sc. 2.

LONDON:

EFFINGHAM WILSON & CO., ROYAL EXCHANGE.

1892.

A Review of the

ECONOMIC POSITION AND LIABILITIES

OF THE

ARGENTINE REPUBLIC.

At the commencement of the year 1889 the various
bonds issued by the National and Provincial Governments of the Argentine Confederation, the Federal and
State Mortgage Banks, and the Municipalities, as well
as those delivered in payment of Public Works and the
bonds and shares of Railway Companies, were collec-
tively valued on the European Stock Exchanges at about
172 millions sterling. At the opening of the year 1891
their value as similarly estimated was 75 millions sterling, showing a decrease in value of about 97 millions.

The President of the Republic in his message of the
9th of May, 1891, to Congress, stated that the losses
within the period referred to, owing to shrinkage in the
value of foreign and home securities quoted on the
Exchange, amounted to not less than 200 millions
sterling, and it may be added that the downward movement has been continued since that date, and that there
has resulted an average fall in the value of Argentine
securities of probably not less than 65 per cent.

The National Government has ceased to pay interest
on its debt (except in the case of one special loan of

A 2

comparatively small amount), or to meet claims on account of the interest it has guaranteed on railway capital expenditure, and the Provincial Governments have followed suit. The dollar bank note, with a nominal value at par of gold of four shillings, and with an exchange value of 3s. 4d. in January, 1889, had fallen in the autumn of 1891 to an exchange value of less than one shilling, imports have decreased by 50 per cent., and the value of real estate is depressed in an equal ratio. The National and State Banks are insolvent, and repayment of deposits has been suspended. The Mortgage Banks instituted by National or Provincial Government decrees have ceased to pay interest on the bonds issued to them by mortgagers, and which represent security for the loans raised on mortgage deeds held by the Banks. In 1889 immigration exceeded emigration by 225,000 persons, but in the first four months of 1891 emigrants have exceeded immigrants by 9,570.

The acute financial and commercial crisis which is pictured in this foregoing short statement of occurrences of recent date is the result not of one, but a variety of causes which have co-operated in bringing it about.

Amongst them may be enumerated the fall in the rate of interest on money in this country, emphasised by the conversion of Consols in 1888, leading to its increased outflow for investment abroad, and facilitating the raising of loans by the Argentine Government; the rapid and astonishing progress of the United States exhibited by enormous increase in population and accumulated wealth, and the belief thus engendered that with the impulse given to the Argentine by the inflow of labour and capital the latent agricultural and pastoral wealth would be rapidly realised, and that extravagance in expenditure and even waste would be

overtaken by the tide of prosperity and might be
disregarded ; the promulgation of a banking and
currency law which was totally unsuited to the character
of the people and their political condition ; the co-part-
nership of the National and Provincial Governments
in the Federal and State Banks, with the natural
result of their interference with the management, and
the distribution of the bank funds in the interests of the
party in power; the use by the Government of enormous
sums raised abroad by way of loans for wildly speculative and illegitimate purposes, through the agency of
the banks, and in fact the general endowment of
numerous institutions of this class with capital so
raised; the maintenance of the inconvertibility of the
paper currency, and the illegal and clandestine issue of
paper money to an amount far in excess of the limit
assigned to each of the banks by law; the creation by
all these means of a mass of currency greatly exceeding
the legitimate needs of the people, and leading inevitably
to its depreciation, to undue inflation of values and
credit, and prodigious speculation of an unsound
character.

The fact that a fall in the average rate of interest
leads to the exportation of capital is too well under-
stood to require explanation or demonstration ; and the
manner in which foreign capital was poured into the
Argentine during the past eight or ten years, and the
general faith expressed in the continuous and rapid
progress of the country, are also matters of common
knowledge and recollection. The connection of the
administrative acts of the Juarez Celman Government
with the condition of affairs as now exhibited is, however,
not so well or so generally known.

The existence of a plethora of capital in England,

and to a less extent in some other European countries, and an unreasonable expectation of the rapid realisation of wealth by the development of the undoubtedly great resources of Argentina (an expectation unquestionably shared by a number of statesmen in the Republic itself), was sufficient to give rise to excessive speculative enterprise in the country; but this movement of capital was greatly stimulated, and the inevitable catastrophe accelerated and intensified, by the passing in 1887 of what is known as "Pacheco's Free Banking and Currency Law."

The unit of currency in the Argentine Confederation is the peso or dollar, a silver coin weighing 385·8 grains. The exigencies of the Government on the one hand and of foreign exchange on the other have led to the practical replacement of the silver dollar in the one case by bank notes with a face value recorded in dollars, and in the other by gold dollars of a value of 4·04 shillings, or practically one-fifth of a pound sterling.

Bank notes have been in use since 1826, and the value of the paper dollar has fluctuated immensely in relation to gold. Greater stability in the terms of interchange transactions and payments has been secured by adopting in many cases the system of making contracts for payment in gold, and these contracts have long been both legally and commercially recognised. Every bill or document which contains an obligation to pay in gold can, however, be liquidated by the delivery of its equivalent in paper currency at the rate of exchange ruling at the time of payment.

The fluctuations which have occurred both recently and during past years in the value of the paper relatively to the gold dollar form such an important factor in any consideration of the Argentine finances, and affect so continually statistical statements in which money values occur, that a brief notice of them is here absolutely necessary, whether for recollection or reference during the perusal of what follows.

The political troubles and wars which desolated the country from 1826 to 1862 rendered a forced paper currency a necessity, and military exigencies caused the printing and issue of notes without the slightest regard for consequences. By 1830 the paper dollar had fallen in value to 6d.; from 1830 to 1837 its average value was 8d., with an issue of 15 million dollars. In 1840 the issue had increased to 50 million dollars, and the value had fallen to 1½d. In 1845 each paper dollar was worth 4d. In 1846 the issue was increased by 80 millions, and the value fell to 2d. In 1852 the issue had further increased to 120 millions, and the value of the dollar was 2½d. In this year Rosas was defeated and driven from the country; but from 1852 to 1861 the issue increased at the rate of 25 millions annually, and at the end of that period the nominal amount was $375,000,000, with an exchange value of 2½d. In 1866 there were actually $430,000,000 paper in circulation, and in the following year the Government authorised the encashment of notes at the rate of 25 paper for one gold dollar, and they were thus put on a metallic basis. In 1876 there was a further fall in the Exchange, when 35 paper dollars had to be given for one gold dollar, and the notes were again made inconvertible.

After 1881 the value of the currency revived, and a law was passed providing for the coinage of gold and silver, and during a brief period of eighteen months from the middle of 1883 to the end of 1884 paper dollars were exchangeable for gold dollars at their face value. In January, 1885, a decree re-establishing forced currency was passed, but it implicitly recognised the validity of contracts for payment in gold.

The value of the paper money was again depreciated. In 1885 the average value of the paper dollar in sterling was 35d., in 1886 31d., in 1887 36d., in 1888 32d., in 1889 27d., in 1890 18d., during the first half of 1891 13d., and in September 1891, 12d.

These fluctuations in the value of the currency, extending over a period of 65 years, have necessarily had an unfavourable effect on the trade of the country, hampering commercial transactions and introducing a speculative element into all the relations of creditor and debtor. These evils have been intensified during the past two years by the violence of the fluctuations occurring within short periods.

The currency and legal tender of the country which should be the standard of value for every commodity has become more unstable in value than any other species of property.

The quantity of money in circulation is a measure of the demand for commodities, and with increased demand prices rise. If the circulating medium of a country consists of gold, the quantity in circulation will constantly tend to become that which will maintain its value relatively to commodities in general, at an equality with the value of gold in other countries estimated on the same basis.

If the value of gold, whether currency or bullion, in any country becomes lower than in other countries—that is to say, if prices in general are higher in any given country than in other countries—there will result an exportation of gold from the country where its value is low to the countries where its value is greater, to be employed in the purchase of commodities which are in consequence relatively cheap. There will follow an importation of commodities, exchanged for the exported gold, and a reduction of the amount of currency which will tend to restore equilibrium between the home and foreign values of gold.

If the circulating medium consists of bank notes convertible on demand into gold, the same tendency of the currency to constancy in general value will exist, or at least a tendency to that level of value which is constantly approached in all commercial countries in consequence of the mobility or fluidity of gold.

The amount of bank notes in circulation cannot exceed that which is consistent with their exchange at par value, because the moment they fell below par they would be returned to the issuing bank and exchanged for gold.

If the circulating medium is of a compound character and consist partly of gold and partly of notes not convertible on demand, the notes will be maintained at their face value in gold, because exportation for profit of the metallic portion of the currency, and its consequent contraction, will take place whenever its value relatively to commodities falls to the point at which such profit can be made.

If when the whole of the metallic portion of the currency has disappeared, circumstances occur, such as the continual issue of paper, or the contraction of trade which render the inconvertible currency redundant, it will circulate at a discount.

Not only will the bank note fail to purchase the amount of gold coin which its face value represents, but it will also fail to purchase the amount of commodities which the gold coin would exchange for. Every fresh issue of paper will then aggravate its depreciation to which there will be no limit ; and the currency can only be restored to par value by reducing the amount of the notes in circulation.

The Argentine paper currency is in the condition described. It is inconvertible and it is redundant. It amounted in June, 1891, to $260,000,000, which at par would represent £52,000,000, or £13 per head of the population of about four millions, the value of whose foreign trade can hardly exceed for 1891 £35,000,000. In Australia the coin and bank notes in circulation are estimated at about £6 per head of the population numbering about 3,400,000, with a foreign trade the volume of which is at least £55,000,000.

The value of the foreign trade of countries such as those mentioned is at any rate a rough measure of the relative amounts of the internal exchanges, and it needs no long consideration of the above facts in order to recognise how immensely the amount of the currency in circulation in Argentina is in excess of that which would coincide with a par value in exchange.

The sterling value of the paper currency at the rate of exchange prevailing in September, 1891, was 13 million pounds, or £3. 5s. per head of the population. This seems to indicate a degree of depreciation considerably in excess of that which would be due to mere redundancy of paper money, and points to the existence of additional causes leading to fall in its value.

The principal of these has no doubt been the apprehension of further large issues of paper, and of legislation impugning the validity of contracts for payment in gold or otherwise destructive of trade and credit. It is easy to understand that when expectation exists of further reduction in the value of the paper currency, each seller of commodities will endeavour to discount the fall for the period during which he may have to hold the paper which he obtains in exchange for what he sells and the decline is thereby accelerated.

Besides this the history of the paper currency reveals periods of collapse in value greatly in excess of that which has taken place during the present crisis, and there exists no doubt a not unreasonable fear that worse phases of the malady are imminent. Under circumstances of general distrust there will be a tendency to hoard gold, and thus even if imported it may disappear from circulation. There are two factors on which the value of the notes in circulation depends. These are the stability of the convention under which they pass from hand to hand as value for goods sold, or service rendered, and the belief which underlies this, that the Government will maintain their value. This convention does not lapse suddenly, nor does the credit of the Government easily disappear. Both are gradually worn out as depreciation proceeds.

With a small population, and a very partially developed country like the Argentine, this decadence takes place much more easily and rapidly than in the case of older countries with larger populations and accumulated wealth. Despondency soon becomes general, and leads to exaggerated distrust and an unreasonable degree of depreciation in the value of all securities.

However much these various causes and the combined action of speculators may operate on and induce fluctuations in exchange, there can be no doubt whatever that the main cause of the depreciation of the inconvertible paper money has been its excessive issue, and that nothing except a contraction of the currency by the withdrawal of the notes, as recommended by Lord Rothschild's Committee, or the steady and large expansion of the volume of home and foreign trade, causing its readier absorption in current transactions, can avail to restore its exchange value.

The principal banks of the Argentine Republic which existed prior to the financial crisis which brought about their insolvency were the Provincial Bank of Buenos Ayres and the National Bank.

The former was founded in 1822, and it has been said that in 1887 it was, as regards its capital and deposits, equal in importance to the Imperial Bank of Germany, and its note issue was greater than the aggregate of all the banks of Scotland. In November, 1890, its capital amounted to $50,000,000 paper, its note circulation was $58,000,000, deposits $140,000,000, its liabilities $320,000,000. It was a Government Bank, and its profits were applied to defraying the expenses of the Government and notoriously in making advances for political purposes.

The National Bank was founded in 1873 by decree of Congress, and in 1890 had also attained great importance. It was a private corporation, but nearly half the shares were held by the Government, and it was practically under Government control. At the time of its fall its nominal capital was $50,000,000, and its balance-sheet showed a note circulation of $96,000,000, deposits $66,000,000—total liabilities, $442,000,000. These were the chief banks of emission. Their notes were legal tender and circulated throughout the Republic. There were other banks in the Provinces connected with the State Government, but their notes had only local currency.

Attached to the National and Provincial Banks are what are called the Mortgage or Hypothecary Banks.

The Hypothecary Bank of the Province of Buenos

Ayres was constituted in 1873. Its business was to issue loans on the security of real estate. These loans took the form of bonds of the Bank to bearer or to name, carried interest, and were redeemable by drawings—the mortgager paying interest and sinking fund to the Bank, which in turn paid the holder of the bond. No loan was to exceed half the assessed value of the property pledged. The mortgager received the bonds, or Cedulas, as they are called, and placed them on the market. The whole property of borrowers remains liable for the debt incurred.

In July, 1886, it was estimated that one-third of the houses and lands in the City and Province of Buenos Ayres was mortgaged to the Bank which had then issued bonds to the nominal amount of $71,000,000. In 1890 its issue had increased to the enormous amount of $300,000,000 paper.

The National Mortgage Bank which was formed towards the end of 1886 had similar functions. Its issue of bonds had reached in 1890 a total of $20,000,000 gold and $86,000,000 paper. These securities were first placed on the European markets in 1882, and are now very largely held there.

The bonds issued by the National and Provincial Mortgage Banks have the guarantee of the respective Governments.

In November, 1887, a banking law was passed which was similar in some respects to that of the United States, but with the important difference that the notes of the Banks of issue had forced instead of optional currency. This law, as it turned out, was fraught with momentous consequences to the country. Its principal provisions were as follows:—

Any company of three or more persons might

establish a bank of emission in any part of the Republic subject to the following conditions :—

The by-laws having been registered the Company was to apply to the Minister of Finance for permission to open the Bank and make the regulated emission of paper money.

The Statutes were to state the amount of capital and other particulars, and the charter must be for a period of not less than ten years. The capital must not be less than one million dollars, and the amount of the issue was limited to 90 per cent. of the capital. The Bank had to deposit in gold the price of Government bonds corresponding in nominal amount to its issue, and thereupon it was to receive notes to an equal amount. The Government bonds were to be redeemable at par in gold and to bear interest at the rate of 4½ per cent., with one per cent. for amortisation by drawings. The coupons of the bonds were payable in gold. The bonds themselves were to be deposited in the Office of the Board of Credit as a guarantee for the notes of the Bank. The interest due on the bonds was to be paid periodically to the Bank.

Banks founded under this law could increase or decrease their issue provided they increased or decreased the amount of the bonds deposited in the same proportion. They were required to set aside 8 per cent. of their profits to form a reserve fund.

Liquidation was to be controlled by Government officers until the whole of the issued notes had been called in. In the event of bankruptcy the bonds were to be sold on the Exchange, and the proceeds were to be applied to the redemption of the bank issue. The holders of the notes were to have a preferential claim to reimbursement.

Notes issued under this law were made legal tender over the whole of the Republic, and were to be received in payment of all taxes.

All the gold received from the banks in exchange for the Government bonds was to be lodged in the National Bank until the 1st January, 1890, after which the Government was at liberty to apply it to the redemption of the foreign debt.

It was officially stated by the President of the Argentine Republic in his message to Congress of the 6th May, 1889, that within twelve months of the passing of the Free Bank Law 15 new banks were incorporated, with an aggregate capital of $200,000,000 paper and a note circulation of $151,000,000. In this last amount, however, there was included the currency which existed prior to the passing of the Act, amounting to $92,000,000, so that the note issue had increased within that period to the extent of 51 per cent. Within the same period the value of the paper dollar relatively to gold had fallen 8 per cent, and this notwithstanding the importation of 45 million dollars gold, equivalent to nine millions sterling, the produce of loans contracted in Europe in order to provide the capital of the Banks, and the rapid expansion of trade and production due to the expenditure of foreign capital on public works, constructed by English and other companies, and also to immigration stimulated by free passages.

Concurrently with the creation of Free Banks under the new law, there was a great enlargement of the system of Land Mortgage Banks.

The comprehensive and wide-spreading character of the machinery which was thus put in motion, for the purpose of creating and expanding credit and speculation may be conceived, when it is stated that one bank alone—that of the Province of Buenos Ayres—had forty branches, and that the total number of distinct banking institutions were also forty, with an aggregate capital of $350,000,000, assets $137,000,000 gold, and $460,000,000 paper, and a note issue of $200,000,000.

In a report to the President of the Republic, dated the 28th February 1889, Señor Pacheco made a number of congratulatory remarks with reference to the effect of the financial policy and measures of the Government as exemplified by the Free Banking Law and the creation of Mortgage Banks. These latter are stated to have mobilised dead capital under the ægis of the Government, and to have enabled landlords to count on personal and genuine credit, to have strengthened the value of land, and stimulated agriculture.

As regards the free banks, it was announced that they had revolutionised the economic system of the country. The 16 free banks being governed by the State under one law, the currency had been unified and placed under the control of the Legislature. It was pointed out that the notes were guaranteed by public bonds, the interest on which was paid in gold, and also by the reserve of 10 per cent. in gold on the amount of the issue of each bank. If these securities did not suffice to pay the value of the note, the State would intervene and provide the balance.

The Minister concluded his remarks on this head by stating that when a forced paper currency is decreed, the note issue necessarily doubles and trebles itself, because it would be absurd to make a people live on an inconvertible currency equal to the disposable amount at the time the currency was convertible, and apparently attributes the rapid increase of wealth in the United States after the war of Secession to the large amount of the inconvertible issues of its banks !

It was into these banks of the Argentine Republic, and chiefly into the National Bank, and the Provincial Bank of the State of Buenos Ayres, that were poured the proceeds of loans raised in Europe. The National and State Governments not only controlled their respective banks in virtue of their executive authority, but they were in the position of partners in these concerns, and participated in the profits arising from their operations.

The National Government held 160,000 shares in the National Bank, the value of which in 1889 was no less than $47,000,000, and yielded a profit of $3,600,000. The same course was followed by the Provincial Governments, who were equally associated with the Banks in their speculations.

Between 1887 and 1890 the amount of mortgage bonds or Cedulas issued by the Mortgage Banks increased from $100,000,000 to $400,000,000, the foreign debt from £48,000,000 to about £73,000,000, and the note issue from $94,000,000 to $300,000,000, while the premium on gold rose from 35 per cent. to 250 per cent.

As has already been explained, various State Governments borrowed money in Europe for the purpose of making the deposit required by the Treasury for the purchase of national gold bonds to guarantee their note issue. In a number of instances, however, the bills of the States were accepted by the National Government in lieu of gold as the consideration for the purchase of the bonds. Nevertheless immense sums in gold were thus transferred to the coffers of the National Bank, by which the money was used in banking and speculative operations, or sold on the Bourse in the vain endeavour to check the continually increasing depreciation of the paper currency. It will have been observed that this

B

gold was pledged by the Free Bank Act for the redemption of the foreign debt.

It is rather the general drift of the finances of the country than accurate details which are to be gathered from the public statements of the Ministers, and from other records. The omission in many of the statements of clear expressions of the nature of the currency in which the details are entered renders them often valueless. When paper dollars are equivalent in purchasing power to a shilling only, while gold dollars are worth four shillings, it is obviously of the greatest importance that it should be explained whether figures, representing assets and liabilities, revenue and expenditure, imports and exports, are expressed in gold or in paper dollars. Yet this is a point which is often left quite indeterminate. It is not the purpose of this paper to give anything like a complete history of the events in the Argentine Republic which culminated in the crash of 1890–91. The materials for such a history doubtless exist, but they are not available in this country. It will suffice if a brief analysis of the financial situation as described by the Ministers at the meeting of Congress in May, 1891, is put before the reader, together with such comments as appear to be necessary in order to explain, as far as may be, the manner in which the proceeds of the numerous loans raised in Europe during recent years have been disposed of, and what the general liabilities and assets of the National and Provincial Governments amount to.

The Financial Minister, Dr. V. .F. Lopez, in his Report of the 5th May, 1891, stated that, on assuming charge of his office in August, 1890, "he found the Treasury empty, and the National and Mortgage Banks and the Municipality of Buenos Ayres, the Federal

Capital, in a state of ruin. The National Bank owed the Treasury 12 million dollars gold and 47½ million dollars paper. It owed besides £3,700,000 in Europe, and 11½ millions dollars gold to creditors in the Argentine. Its assets were for the most part worthless, or at the moment unrealisable. The National Mortgage Bank owed $1,700,000 paper and $550,000 gold.

" The Municipality of Buenos Ayres was in debt to the extent of 34,650,000 paper dollars and 10,270,000 gold dollars. The books of the National Bank had been kept so flagrantly that it was impossible to arrive at its losses, or to gain a clear view of its liabilities in the Argentine or in Europe. The Provincial Bank of Buenos Ayres was found to be in a hopeless condition, and had had recourse to clandestine issues of paper money; its funds had been wasted in colossal enterprises and undue liberality of discounts. It was maintained by a system of unlimited issues of currency. The Mortgage Bank of the Province had got into such difficulties that it suspended payment of the coupons of its bonds in March, 1891. All the Provinces were bankrupt, and suspended payment with liabilities which, exclusive of those of the Province of Buenos Ayres, amounted to nearly 100 million gold dollars. Efforts were made to save the banks and municipality from default by the issue of 60 million paper dollars "—a course admitted to be only justified under the pressure of a terrible necessity —" and by raising an internal loan by public subscription, but without success, and the banks were closed by decree of the Government on the 7th April, 1891."

The foregoing remarkable statements were supplemented a few days later by some observations of the

President, Dr. Pellegrini, in his Message to the Legislature. He announced that the gold reserves in the National Bank had been sold for paper currency at a loss of 150 per cent.—this included the fund guaranteeing the note circulation—and that the National Bank and the Provincial Bank of Buenos Ayres had prevailed on the former President of the Republic to make a clandestine issue of paper amounting to 26 million dollars for the National Bank and 8,700,000 dollars for the Provincial Bank, in order to stave off default.

In consequence of the disastrous condition of the National Bank, a new Board was appointed in 1890, which proceeded to investigate its affairs, and which on the 7th April, 1891, presented a report to the Government (which had replaced that of Sr. Juarez Celman). No more uncompromising statement of nefarious financial transactions has ever been penned. A pithy and terse extract was published by the *Buenos Ayres Standard* of the 29th of April following, which states :

" Bank and Government have marched hand in
" hand. All laws and privileges granted by the latter
" having served to draw closer the connection between
" them. Results :—Loans to members of Government,
" to all kinds of politicians whose liabilities have not
" been met, and whose assets are illusory. Invest-
" ment of bank funds in stock speculations, advances at
" long dates, loans to the Government to meet ordinary
" expenditure ; payment of interest on these a dead
" letter or very irregular. Purchase of fraudulent
" Provincial paper issues. Purchase of Provincial
" bonds—a dead loss to the Bank. Purchase of
" national loans for the construction of railways at
" high quotations. Purchase of companies' stocks, an
" operation outside the limits of bank business, which

" have entailed considerable losses. Intrusion of the
" Government which had direct and unquestioned
" control over the internal management of the Bank.
" Violation of bank secrets. A prominent member of
" the Government used to enter the Bank and give
" orders over the heads of all directors and managers
" for the delivery of large sums to individuals. Com-
" plete mismanagement and utter disorder in the internal
" administration of affairs. Acceptance of drafts by
" employés of the Bank for amounts twenty or thirty
" times larger than those authorised by the Board of
" Managememt, which are still unpaid. Appropriation
" of Bank funds for speculative purposes. Loans to
" third parties whose operations showed that they were
" for account of those who granted the money. Appro-
" priation of the Bank funds by managers of branches
" with a view to operating on their own account, or of
" lending to concerns in which they were interested.
" Utter absence of an index to the records, and a vast
" accumulation of documents which baffle classification
" and investigation. No supervision of accounts either
" in head office or in branches. Managers and clerks
" engaged in speculative enterprises. False balance-
" sheets prepared, and illusory dividends distributed.
" The account of bad debts not kept for a long time."

On the 12th June, 1891, a body of special commis-
sioners, who had been appointed for the purpose, made a
further report on the condition of the National Bank
which fully confirmed the statements of the reformed
Board of Directors already quoted. Advances had been
made to the extent of $205,000,000 ; $5,800,000 gold
had been given out amongst 125 persons who were then
indebted to the Bank, and $177,000,000 paper amongst

19,317 persons whose bills were in the Bank Portfolio.
208 persons received advances the aggregate of which
far exceeded the capital of the Bank. The Directors
found it necessary in 1890 to write off $27,000,000
currency as irrecoverable. In loans to provinces and
advances to banks the Bank locked up $34,000,000
gold.

The commission sum up their report in the following
words:—

" After a careful study of the books we look in vain
" for the benefits such an institution ought to have
" bestowed on the country. With a heavy heart we find
" an immense amount of stocks and scrip that can only
" become of any value in the remote future. We make
" every allowance for the crisis, but cannot shut our
" eyes to those culpable acts above enumerated which
" have brought the National Bank to its present state.
" Not only the Government, but individuals holding
" public offices were allowed by the Directors to make
" free with the Bank until all respect was lost, and it
" was made a tool for political wire-pulling. The spirit
" of gambling also got into the Bank and pervaded all
" its arteries. The wildest speculations were got up
" actually among the persons to whom the administra-
" tion of the Bank was confided. In the meantime
" confusion reigned in every department; bills were
" abandoned, wrong balance-sheets were drawn up,
" and imaginary dividends were distributed amongst
" the shareholders." *

Reports made with reference to the Provincial Bank of
Buenos Ayres and the Banks of the Provinces disclosed
conditions equally disastrous with those of the National

* Foreign Office Report, March, 1892.

Bank. The collective liabilities of the National and State banks probably amount to not less than 700 million dollars paper.

Their assets are represented by an enormous mass of securities which are either seriously depreciated or valueless. The task of liquidation, which as yet appears hardly to have been touched, will be a gigantic one. In the interests of the creditors it is urgent, for it is to be supposed that much of the property of debtors which is at first tangible does not long remain so if sequestration is delayed.

These remarks apply with equal force to the Hypothecary Banks, which have accepted mortgages to the enormous amount of 806 million dollars paper, and 24,600,000 dollars gold, carrying interest amounting to $29,000,000 paper, and $1,230,000 gold, on the greater part of which default has been made. These advances, made for the most part during a period when land had attained highly inflated values and speculation was rife, are, to say the least, in many cases insufficiently secured.

An Argentine estimate classes 35 per cent. of them as well guaranteed, 17 per cent. partially guaranteed, and 48 per cent. worthless. ¦

One must assume that the political exigencies of the time required the publication of the Bank Commission Report, and the delivery by the Ministers and President in Congress of the foregoing remarkable statements as to the history and condition of the banks of issue generally. It may be that these statements are highly coloured, and that liquidation would show better results than is now anticipated. Nevertheless the effect of such utterances on public opinion, and particularly European opinion, must be reckoned with. Not only was the credit of these particular institutions utterly shattered, but their rehabilitation was rendered impossible. It seems to be the intention of the Government to merge the functions of the National and Provincial Banks in one establishment, and in fact the so-called "Banco Unico,' has been created by decree of the Legislature for that purpose. It has been endowed with funds by an issue of paper currency, of course-at the expense of every holder of notes of the previous issues whose capital is *pro tanto* depreciated. But European capital will hardly be entrusted to the Bank, nor does it seem probable that the savings of natives or foreigners will ¡be deposited there, in view of the fate of depositors in the moribund banks of the State. The reproductive power of the country is undeniably very great, and the value of real property must before long recover from its present extreme depression. A certain amount of quiet investment by private persons is in progress, but this cannot affect the immense amount of property pledged to the National and Provincial banks, and to their satellites, the Mortgage banks, until liquidation is in satisfactory progress ; and not even then unless European capital is at hand, under skilful management, and on a considerable scale, to stimulate prices, establish confidence, and create a demand for the property in the hands of the liquidators. It is natural that the national pride of the Argentines should lead them to object to any proposals that the funds of the national treasury should be managed by a bank under the control of foreigners ; but it would be unwise on their part not to make in other respects all possible allowances for the distrust quite as naturally inspired in Europe, by the revelations of their own Ministers in Congress, and thus preclude the co-operation of European capitalists in the task of recon-

structing credit, and minimising the sacrifices and
sufferings which must necessarily to some extent be
endured.

Many published statements have appeared purport-
ing to give an account of the indebtedness of the
National and Provincial Governments of the Republic,
but they have differed more or less widely from each
other, and but limited confidence can be placed in any
of them.

The various statements of the Ministers and officials
have lacked precision and detail, and this is hardly sur-
prising when the irregularities which have been revealed
are taken into consideration.

The rapid distribution of the millions (sent during
the past seven or eight years to the Argentine from
Europe) through the innumerable channels, legitimate
or illegitimate, kept open by the banks, accompanied as
it was by incompleteness and extreme laxity in book-
keeping, renders it hopeless at present to attempt to
estimate the value of the assets which would be available in reduction of the liabilities of the Government.

Besides this it has to be considered that the debts
contracted in paper currency are subject to enormous
fluctuation in the amount when referred to the gold
standard.

During 1889 a pound sterling was exchanged on the
average for eight paper dollars; but during 1891 the
pound would on the average have purchased 19 paper
dollars. The Government now collect the main portion
of the revenue in gold, or at least in paper dollars
equivalent at the current rate of exchange to the amount
of the taxes estimated in gold. Their resources are
based on production, the products having a tolerably
constant gold value. It is clear that in such an opera-

tion, for instance, as the redemption of the paper currency to such an extent as to cause its restoration to par of gold, the outlay necessary would be the value in gold of the paper which could be purchased below par, at the average rate of exchange at which purchases were made. No one can say how much currency could be so redeemed before the exchange rose to par. When the paper dollar was exchangeable for a gold dollar, there would be no necessity for further contraction of the bank note circulation, and probably this condition would be attained on the withdrawal of much less than half the paper now in circulation. Expansion of trade and internal interchanges would raise the exchange value of the paper dollar irrespective of its redemption.

Considering the rapid and large fluctuations in the liabilities of the Government as estimated in gold, due to the circumstances above described, absolute precision in any general statement of the debt of the nation is of little moment. The following *résumé* of the debt has been compiled from the best sources available.

[*See opposite page*, 27.]

If the Railway Interest Guarantee for terms of years is capitalised at 4 per cent., the debt in gold dollars will be increased by $52,425,000, and the total interest reduced by $2,403,000 gold. In short the Government could equitably discharge their liability in respect of guaranteed interest by an immediate payment of about ten and a half millions sterling, and might be supposed, on the other hand, to lose the interest realisable on the capital parted with.

The National Government have issued about $164,000,000 gold bonds to guarantee the note issue of the State banks. These are lodged in the office of

APPROXIMATE ESTIMATE of the Liabilities of the National and Provincial Governments and the Municipalities of the Argentine Republic on the 31st December, 1891.

	Debt contracted in Gold.	Debt contracted in Paper.	Exclusive of Sinking Fund — Annual Interest on Gold Debt.	Exclusive of Sinking Fund — Annual Interest on Paper Debt.
	$	$	$	$
FOREIGN DEBT.				
National ...	104,554,650	.....	9,657,990	.....
Guaranteed Interest on Railways	.....	.....	4,500,000	.....
Municipal and Provincial	161,766,150	.....	9,478,080	.....
Total Foreign Debt ...	266,519,400	.....	23,635,970	.....
INTERNAL DEBT.				
National ...	92,000,000	440,000,000	1,881,064	9,669,048
Provincial and Municipal	18,000,000	575,000,000	693,531	59,350,476
Total ...	45,000,000	819,000,000	2,574,610	50,149,024
Total (Foreign and Internal)	576,019,400	819,000,000	28,010,580	89,149,024

Total as above reduced to pounds sterling on the basis of a Gold Premium of 244 % ...	£121,000,000	£7,904,567
Total, exclusive of liabilities on accounts of Currency and Cedula Banks ...	£161,019,400 (Total, Gold ...) 118,000,000 (Total, Paper ...)	£4,881,070 (Gold) £4,965,000 (Paper)
Total as above reduced to pounds sterling on the basis of a Gold Premium of 251 % ...	£77,000,000	£4,864,184

Currency Conversion, and interest at 4½ per cent. was paid to the banks. The banks purchased these bonds partly with cash and partly by bills. The transactions involved are entirely between the Provincial and the National Government, except as respects $8,000,000 gold received by the latter from the private native and foreign banks in Buenos Ayres, who elected for incorporation under the Free Bank Law. With this exception the item is excluded from the capital statement as the liability is not one which concerns the creditors of the Government except contingently.

Against the liabilities in respect of currency and Cedulas there are assets of unknown value in the shape of discounted bills in the Bank portfolios and the property of mortgagers to the hypothecary banks. The Government guarantee represents collateral security.

In their Nineteenth Annual Report the Corporation of Foreign Bondholders have given a table showing details and a summary of the Argentine External Loans. From the point of view of the writer the table requires alteration in the following particulars, if a fair view of the liabilities of the Nation in comparison with its assets and productive power is to be obtained :—

A sum of £16,000,000, representing the capitalisation of the National Railway guarantees, has been entered as a liability of the Government, and at the same time the full amount of interest (£921,000), guaranteed for terms of years, has been charged against them under the head of "Annual Service of Debt." There does not appear to be any capital liability whatever, and the £16,000,000 in question has been excluded from the writer's estimate of the debt.

In the same table interest seems to have been charged on the original amount of the loans, and not on

the present amount. Specific loans having been largely
reduced by redemption, the amount shown as necessary
for the service of the debt has been unduly swollen by
the method of calculation adopted. Again, the amount
shown for the annual service of the debt includes payments to the sinking fund. In the calculation of debt
service for the purpose of this paper the amounts for
the several sinking funds have been excluded, seeing
that they do not represent liabilities which should be
opposed to resources in a consideration of the question of
solvency. Interest also has been limited to that due
on the present amount of the several loans.

In the Report is a statement of the total debt of the
Argentine Republic, derived from the *Buenos Ayres
Standard* of October, the 22nd and 23rd, 1891, and
compiled by Mr. Mulhall.

In this statement the course followed as regards
Guaranteed Railways was the same as that adopted in
the Table above alluded to, involving the inclusion of a
sum of £16,000,000 as a debt of the Argentine Government, such debt having no existence in fact. In the
same statement a sum of £42,500,000 has been charged
against the Government on account of " Free Bank
Loans," while the liabilities of the Provincial Governments have been reduced on account of gold paid into
the National Treasury to guarantee the note issues of
their banks by £15,000,000.

In view of the fact that the 4½ per cent. of gold
bonds issued by the National Government to guarantee
the note issue, have not been floated so far as is known,
and are simply lodged in a public office, and that if sold
the proceeds are by law only applicable to the redemption of the paper currency (charged in full in the statement against the Government), it is not apparent how

any liability on account of these bonds can be said to exist at the present moment, which is not alternatively represented in the statement of liabilities framed by the writer, under the heads either of Foreign Provincial loans, the service of such loans, or currency. If by the term Free Bank Loans is not meant the gold bonds referred to, but some other liability adopted by the Government in connection with the banks, it cannot equitably be charged without also taking the Bank assets into account.

The National Government has guaranteed the deposits in the banks of Buenos Ayres and the National Bank closed by decree in 1891. There are liabilities also in the shape of guarantees on sugar and meat factories, the amount of which is unknown. The bank assets will be available to some extent when realised for the payment of depositors. But the whole position in this respect is too chaotic to deal with.

It is obviously quite impracticable at present to form any estimate whatever of the value of the assets of the National and Provincial Governments which might be available in liquidation. Theoretically, of course, the resources of the country are pledged to the creditors, and it is on their development and on honest administration that the future ability of the Government to fulfil their engagements wholly depends.

From the foregoing statement it will be seen that the foreign debt—National, Provincial, and Municipal—is approximately £66,000,000, with an annual charge for interest, including railway guarantees of £4,727,000. The total debt, external and internal (exclusive of the liabilities on account of Cedulas and currency), calculated on the basis of a gold premium of 254 per cent., amounts to £77,000,000, with annual charge for interest of £5,400,000.

The imposition and collection of taxes on imports and exports in gold is a perfectly legitimate proceeding, seeing that products have a value in gold which is determined by European prices. It would be equally equitable to levy the land tax in gold. The exclusion from present consideration of the currency as part of the debt of the National Government may be justified by the fact that there never could be any occasion for redeeming by purchase more than a portion of it, and because even that portion might be left in circulation without much embarrassment, if only the political condition of the country were stable, and the financial policy of the Government honest, wise, and unchangeable. Under such circumstances the fluctuation in the exchange value of the currency would be immeasurably reduced in amplitude, and prices and wages would accommodate themselves to the circumstances which would have little variation. It is the rapid and violent changes in the value of the currency in reference to gold, and therefore to commodities in general due to uncertainty and wild legislation, which are so embarrassing and disastrous.

Here it may be pointed out, paradoxical as it may seem, that the issue of 50 millions paper currency, in connection with the creation of the Banco Unico in the Argentine, to supersede the defaulting banks, will in all probability not increase the real burden of the Government in respect of currency. The value in gold of the inconvertible paper currency in the mass is practically determined by the demand for the paper as a medium of exchange and by the credit of the Government, and it does not matter as regards that gross value in gold how many counters in the shape of paper dollars the mass is represented by. If the number of counters is increased, the value of each will decrease ultimately in the same ratio if the demand and the credit of the Government continue unchanged.

It would probably cost the Government no more in gold to bring a paper currency of $300,000,000 to par by the purchase of the paper in the market than it would to effect the same change in the case of an issue of $250,000,000. The power of issuing inconvertible notes arms the Government with a most powerful engine of taxation which is put into operation with dangerous ease. When depreciation has set in every fresh issue aggravates the evil, and is in fact the means of extracting from every one holding a note a portion of the value of that which he holds.

The adoption of this means of meeting the liabilities of the Government is as immoral as would be the issue of debentures ostensibly secured on real estate, and made to rank with a previous issue which had been accepted on the faith of a declaration of its priority as a charge on the same estate.

We have seen in the course of the foregoing account that the Government of Juarez Celman, and also the Provincial Governments of the Argentine, adopted the *rôle* of Bankers and speculators, as well as that of Administrators.

In the latter capacity they raised loans in the money markets of Europe in the name of the nation. In the former they dealt with the money entrusted to them in the manner which has been described.

No doubt large sums have been expended for perfectly legitimate purposes, and with great benefit to the country. Subventions to railway companies, taking the form of guaranteed interest, and outlay in assisting immigration, on harbours, railways, and public works of a reproductive character, are amply justified; but, on the other hand, many millions have been squandered in speculative enterprises which no Government should touch, or distributed amongst members of the late Government and their friends, under cover of bill transactions of the most transparent kind. The interest on loans has been met by fresh borrowing or paid out of banking profits which were in turn illusory.

The financial situation is sufficiently serious, but a consideration of the character of the country and its resources, and especially the extraordinary progress which it has made during the past fifteen years, affords reasonable ground for the expectation that material recovery cannot be long delayed.

In respect of climate, and pastoral and agricultural capabilities, there is much resemblance between the Argentine Republic and Australia. The populations of the two countries are not widely different in numbers, and much may be learnt from a comparative study of the progress of each during recent times.

The area of the territory of the Republic is about 1,100,000 square miles, or nine times that of Great Britain and Ireland. The area of Australia is estimated at 3,000,000 square miles.

In the interior of either country there are vast tracts which are arid and uncultivable ; the limits of profitable occupation for both pastoral and agricultural purposes being practically determined in both cases by the distance from the coast to which the area of sufficient average annual rainfall extends. There are fertile tracts in each the aggregate area of which is several times that of the United Kingdom, and no doubt capable of supporting as dense a population.

Australia stretches north and south through 27 degrees of latitude, and two-fifths of its area lies within the tropics. The Argentine territory touches on the north the southern tropic, and extends southwards through 30 degrees of latitude.

The climates of the two countries vary of course to a corresponding extent, that is to say, from temperate to tropical or sub-tropical, and production has an equally wide range in kind and variety.

It might probably be assumed for purposes of comparison that, other things being equal, the capacities of populations for bearing the burden of public debt are measured in each case by the ratio of the value of the surplus production to the amount of the debt, the term surplus production being taken to mean the balance available after the necessary costs of subsistence and of government have been met. A question is here represented which necessarily intrudes itself, but which unfortunately can never be fully solved from prior considerations. It may be more simply stated by saying that the capacity of populations for paying their debts is measured by the amount of taxation which they will endure. Nevertheless it will be useful to estimate the value of the annual production of Australia and Argentina respectively, and to compare the factors influencing production, the liabilities of the two countries, and their taxation and revenue, which last is an index to the cost of administration.

Argentine statistics rest upon too uncertain a basis to be introduced into any comparative statement without premising that large allowance must be made for errors and misstatements. Nevertheless, if duly examined and used with caution, they no doubt form a sufficiently sound foundation on which to rest broad conclusions.

The population and the number of miles of railway

open in the years 1869 and 1889 in Australia and the Argentine respectively are shown in the following statement:—

	1869.		1889.	
	AUSTRALIA.	ARGENTINE.	AUSTRALIA	ARGENTINE
Population	1,517,000	1,730,000	3,015,000	4,100,000
Miles of Railway open	940	480	8,600	5,000

Comparing now other factors influencing production we have for 1889 the following:—

	AUSTRALIA.	ARGENTINE.
Area under cultivation ......Acres	7,082,000	8,800,000
Live Stock ....Sheep	84,800,000	86,400,000
,, ...Horned Cattle	8,500,000	25,800,000
,, ...Horses	1,587,000	4,290,000

A careful examination of the published statistics of the two countries leads to the conclusion that while the total annual value of Australian products—agricultural, pastoral, mining, and manufacturing—amounts to not less than £77,000,000, the gross yearly value of the production of the Argentine may be taken at £45,000,000.

As regards population and the mere numbers of live stock of various kinds existing in the country, the Argentine Republic would appear from the foregoing statement to be in a better position than Australia, there being an excess in the former of 18,000,000 horned cattle and nearly 8,000,000 horses. The area cultivated in Australia in 1889 did not exceed that cultivated in the Argentine by more than 16 per cent. The statistics of the agricultural and pastoral productions of the two countries show, however, that while as respects the first they are practically on an equality, the pastoral production of Australia is far in excess of that of the Argentine.

The value of the annual wool clip of the former is estimated at from 18 to 22 millions sterling, while that of the latter does not exceed seven to eight millions sterling. The reasons assigned by the most competent authorities for this comparatively small production are various. It is stated that the sheep originally introduced into Argentina were far inferior to those which originated the flocks of Australia, and that the former were further injured by inbreeding. Although that cause of deterioration has in general ceased to exist, and much fresh blood of the best quality has been introduced into the Argentine territory within the past ten years, other circumstances react unfavourably on the pastoral industry. Many of the sheep are in the hands of small owners, who have neither the intelligence nor the capital to carry on the business after the best system, or to introduce the breeds best suited to the climate and soil of the various Provinces, whereas the exact contrary is the case in Australia.

A real and extensive evil in Argentina is the prevalence of scab amongst the sheep, due to the absence of legislation for the prevention of the contact of diseased and healthy flocks. It is obvious that there is room for vast improvements and immense increase in the value of the Argentine flocks and the annual production therefrom. The same may be said of the cattle industry, in which the waste is now enormous, owing to the at present unmarketable character of the larger portion of

each animal slaughtered. These difficulties in the way
of the utilisation in Europe of the food supplies of the
Argentine are being overcome, and, as a matter of fact,
fat bullocks three years old, sold at 30s. per head in that
country, were landed at Liverpool in 1891 and sold for
slaughter at £18 per head.

The mining and manufacturing industries in the
Argentine are in their infancy—in fact the former can
hardly be said to exist.

While the whole production of Australia amounts in
value to nearly £36 per head of the population, that of
the Argentine does not appear to exceed £12 per head.
The relations of the production of the two countries to
their debt and to the revenue of the Governments are
dealt with further on.

The construction of railways in the Argentine has
made remarkable progress within the past twenty years,
and to this is mainly due the rapid development of the
country and the great increase in general and especially
agricultural production. Continuing the comparison
already entered on of Australian and Argentine statistics, we find that in the former there were in 1869
about 950 miles of line open and in the latter 450 miles.
At the end of 1889 the Australian Colonies had
constructed 8,600 miles of railway and the Argentine
Republic 5,088 miles. It will be seen that the length of
railways constructed in Australia was nine times and
in the Argentine eleven times as great as it was in the
respective countries at the commencement of the period
included.

This, however, by no means represents the state of
affairs in the Argentine at the present time, for progress
in construction has been accelerated. On the 31st
March, 1891, there were 7,190 miles of railway in

operation, with an actual outlay on lines working or under construction of £60,000,000; by far the greater portion of which represents British capital. The length of the lines under survey or construction was 7,370 miles, and the liabilities of the Government in respect of guaranteed interest amounted to £900,000 per annum.

The following statement shows the relations of the railways in the two countries as regards equipment, traffic, cost, and other details so far as these can be arrived at with the information available.

1889.	ARGENTINE.	AUSTRALIA.	
Number of Locomotives per mile open	0·150	0·210	
„ Passenger Carriages „	0·225	0·431	VICTORIA.
„ Goods Wagons „	3·84	3·99	
„ Passengers „	2,192	32,188	
„ Tons Goods „	1,333	1,940	
Gross Receipts per train mile	4s.	5s. 9d.	
Capital cost per mile	£9,500	£10,000	
Gross Earnings per mile per annum ..	£881	£884	
Expenses „ „ ...	£621	£546	
Net Profit „ „ ...	£260	£338	
Proportion of net Earnings to capital cost per cent.	2·60	3·55	
„ Expenses to Gross Revenue per cent.	70·7	61·8	

It must be noted that the net profits in gold of the Argentine railways have been subjected to considerable reduction since 1889, in consequence of the continual depreciation of the paper currency, which has been so rapid that the companies have not been able to compensate themselves by the periodical increase in their

charges which they are authorised under such circumstances to make.

The Argentine railways have been built on two
gauges—the one 5 feet 6 inches, and the other one
metre; the Australian railways on three gauges—5 feet
3 inches, 4 feet 8½ inches, and 3 feet 6 inches. Under
these circumstances the relative cost of the railways in
the two countries may be fairly compared since the
average efficiency of the system of one country would
probably not be widely different from that of the system
of the other.

It is evident from the foregoing statement that the
passenger traffic on the Argentine railways is insignificant when compared with that which exists on the
railways of the Australian Colonies.

The revenue of the former is mainly derived from
goods traffic, and approximates closely per mile open to
that of the latter. Nevertheless the tonnage of goods
carried per mile is smallest in the case of the Argentine
railways, and it is a necessary deduction that the tariff
for goods must be far higher in the Argentine than in
Australia.

The net revenue and the proportion of the gross
revenue expended in working in the case of the Argentine railways compare unfavourably with the results
obtained on the Australian railways, and the general
return on the capital expended is at present unsatisfactory.

These remarks refer, of course, to the average results
obtained in 1889 from the working of the whole system of
railways constructed in the Argentine Republic, and are
not inconsistent with the fact that the railways of two or
three companies, and notably the Buenos Ayres and
Great Southern Company, showed large percentages of

profits on working. These are exceptions to the general rule.

That portion of the territory of the Argentine Republic which has been opened up to a very considerable extent by railways forms a tolerably compact block with an area of about 517,000 square miles. It is bounded on the south by a line 600 miles in length drawn in a north-westerly direction from Bahia Blanca on the coast to the Andes in the latitude of Mendoza, on the west by another line drawn from the last-mentioned point to Jujuy in the north, a distance of 670 miles.

The northern boundary, which is very irregular, runs from near Jujuy parallel to the Rio Salado, and about thirty miles to the east of it, in a south-easterly direction to the parallel of 29° south latitude, thence to the town of Corrientes on the Paraguay; again east for 120 miles in Paraguay until it strikes the River Uruguay. Disregarding the Uruguayan territory, which has a system of railways of its own, the boundary of the Argentine country fairly opened up by railways is completed by following the River Uruguay to the estuary of the Plate and continuing along the coast to Bahia Blanca. Within practically the whole of the area included, which is five times the extent of the United Kingdom, there will soon be very few places where the value of land and economic production will not be greatly enhanced by the railway system.

In respect of fertility and resources this area, which is indicated on the small map facing the first page by shading, comprises the most favoured portions of the Argentine Confederated States. There are within it only about 480 inhabitants to every mile of railway as compared with 1,910 in the United Kingdom, 2,061 in

Germany, 2,121 in France, and a population not exceeding seven persons to the square mile, contrasted with populations of 815 to the square mile in the United Kingdom, 824 in Germany, and 187 in France.

When considering the facilities for internal communication, created almost wholly by British capital, within the region in question, those bestowed to a lavish extent by nature must not be forgotten.

The waterways provided by the River Plate and its tributaries, the Parana, the Uruguay, and the Paraguay, and navigable by large steamers, have an aggregate length of over 2,000 miles, while many hundreds of miles in addition are open to vessels of smaller size.

It is shown by the foregoing statement that between 1869 and 1880 the population of the Argentine was increased by 2,470,000 persons, or to the extent of 191 per cent. The immigration returns extending over this period lead to the conclusion that of this increase 1,000,000 was due to immigration, representing in fact the excess of immigration over emigration. The increase of the Australian population during the same period amounted to 1,544,000, or about 105 per cent. The excess of immigration over emigration accounted, it would appear, for about 50 per cent. of this increase.

It is impossible to ascertain what amount has been expended by the Argentine Government by way of assisted or free passages to immigrants.

It must be something very considerable. The advances made for this purpose between November, 1887, and June, 1891, amounted to $5,000,000, most of which was found to be irrecoverable. It is understood that all expenditure under this head has now ceased.

It has been recently asserted by the officials in charge of the immigration department that outlay has been in the past excessive and indiscriminate, and that a considerable number of unsuitable persons were introduced into the country under the system of free passages. The fact, however, seems to be undoubted that 80 per cent. of the immigrants were of the unassisted class, and 60 per cent. of the whole were agricultural labourers, and therefore well suited to the circumstances of the country.

When instituting a comparison between the economic progress of Australia and that of the Argentine during the past fifteen or twenty years, it is of course necessary that such factors as are represented by the relative increases or decreases in exports, imports, customs revenue, total revenue, and expenditure, and so on, should be considered. The difficulties met with in obtaining figures which can be legitimately contrasted are very considerable. In the first place the statistics of Australian trade include interchanges between the several colonies of the continent; but it is necessary that these should be separated from the interchanges with colonies and countries outside Australia, with a view to the comparison of the latter with the statistics of Argentine trade, which relate wholly to foreign imports and exports abroad. This separation is not easily effected, and the results can only be regarded as approximate.

Again, no comparison of the revenue and expenditure of the Argentine with the revenue and expenditure of Australia would be satisfactory which did not include in the former case the Provincial as well as the National revenue and expenditure.

The information available with reference to the finances of the Provinces is both meagre and unsatisfactory, and the official statements cannot be utilised

	1869.		1889.	
	AUSTRALIA.	AMOUNT.	AUSTRALIA.	AMOUNT.
		£		£
Population ...	1,517,000	1,590,000	8,015,000	4,100,000
Imports exclusive of Gold and Specie	18,000,000	7,000,000	82,000,000	82,000,000*
Imports of Gold and Specie ...	500,000	......	500,000	2,800,000
Exports exclusive of Gold and Specie	12,000,000	5,000,000	98,000,000	18,000,000
Exports of Gold and Specie ...	14,000,000	......	8,600,000	8,600,000
Customs Revenue ...	2,780,000	......	7,000,000	5,300,000
Ordinary Revenue—(National, Provincial, and Municipal) ...	8,865,000	8,500,000	27,000,000	14,000,000
Ordinary Expenditure—(National, Provincial, and Municipal) ...	9,800,000	4,000,000	27,000,000*	18,000,000*
Debt ...	26,000,000	18,000,000	187,000,000	103,000,000
Service of Debt ...	1,164,000	780,000	8,700,000	6,900,000†
Debt, exclusive of liabilities on account of Cedules and Currency ...	...	18,000,000	......	74,000,000
Service of Debt as above ...	...	......	......	8,100,000
Tonnage entered and cleared ...	8,774,000	3,380,000	18,888,000	12,880,000

* Exclusive of Reproduction unless specified here.
† Includes the amount payable on account of guaranteed interest on Railways

without making large reservations for inaccuracy. It is moreover well known that doubts have been thrown on the statements of exports and imports issued by authority.

Under these circumstances the figures in the foregoing statement, so far as they relate to the Argentine, although they have been adopted after the most careful consideration, must be taken with due reserve. They are, however, believed to be sufficiently accurate to form the basis of conclusions of a general character.

It will be seen from the above table that Australia entered the earlier period of which statistics are given with a volume of trade representing an annual value of £30,000,000. There was in 1869 an export of gold in excess of imports of £8,000,000, which should be included, as it was a product of the mines of the country, and therefore the external trade may be taken at £38,000,000. This had expanded in 1889 to £58,000,000, an increase of nearly 74 per cent. During the same period the trade of the Argentine had expanded from a value of £12,000,000 to a value of about £50,000,000, representing an increase of about 300 per cent. The ordinary revenue of the Australian Colonies shows an increase between 1869 and 1889 of 204 per cent.; that of the Argentine during the same period an increase of nearly 300 per cent.

In the matter of increase of indebtedness the Argentine unfortunately maintains this supremacy. Her total debt in 1889 was nine times, or if Cedulas and currency are excluded, six and a half times that of 1869. During the same period Australia had multiplied her debt by five. Of late years the enormous additional expenditure incurred annually in the former country under the authority of special laws has converted the system of Budgets into a farce.

The opinion may be held that since the year 1889 was in the Argentine one of inflation, in common with the others immediately preceding it, any estimate of the rate of expansion of trade and revenue which is based on the returns of that year must be an exaggerated one.

Unquestionably some allowance must be made for the extraordinary impulse given at the time in question to production and interchange by an expenditure of capital which could not possibly be sustained. On the other hand it would be a grave error to assume that the economic factors which measure the wealth and resources of the country are at the present time at their normal dimensions, seeing that what is probably the lowest depths of a phase of depression have been reached. The same remarks apply indeed to the Australian Colonies, which have lapsed from their position of great prosperity in 1889 to one of considerable financial distress at the present time.

During the past twenty years the exportation of pastoral products from the Argentine has increased 40 per cent. An export trade in cereals amounting now to a value of about 5½ millions sterling per annum and in manufactured products to 1¾ millions per annum has been created, and up to the present time the financial crisis seems to have had no effect on exports, which continue to be shipped in full volume. It is true that the return of imports of the first half of 1891 has shown a decrease of 50 per cent. compared with those of 1890 for a similar period, but this is not an evil unmixed with good.

So far as such change is due to decrease in the importation of agricultural and other machinery, and raw or partially manufactured materials and other aids to production, it is to be regretted; but it is also in a

great degree attributable to suspension of the use of
luxuries, such as wine, beer, expensive clothing, and
carriages, and to a check in the construction of build-
ings, both public and private, of extravagant dimensions
and costly imported materials, all of which represented
the employment of capital and labour in a manner so
far useless that it did not aid in the development of the
exportable wealth of the country.

After making every allowance for the results of
inflation and the looseness and ambiguity often mani-
fested by Argentine statistics, there seems to be no
doubt that the progress of the country in development
during the twenty years ending with 1889 had been
most remarkable and of good augury for the future.
As regards extraordinary expenditure and the accumulation of debt, it was, however, far otherwise, and it is
certain that the growth of the ordinary revenue, however
satisfactory in the abstract, had fallen far short of that
which would have supplied a justification for the
enormous borrowing effected in Europe within a few
years by the National and Provincial Governments.

While the ordinary revenue of the country had
increased during twenty years to the extent of 300 per
cent., the debt including collateral liabilities had
increased during the same period by 800 per cent., or if
collateral liabilities are excluded, by 550 per cent.

Much has been heard recently of the debt of
Australia, but in this case an increase of the ordinary
revenue between 1869 and 1889 of 204 per cent. has
been accompanied by an increase of debt of 389 per
cent.—a disproportion quite insignificant when compared
with the case of the Argentine Republic, if all her
liabilities are taken into consideration.

Moreover 83 per cent. of the Australian debt

represents money expended on railways and other public works yielding direct revenue, and 10 per cent. expenditure on works of public utility and on immigration. This expenditure has borne fruit, inasmuch as 40 per cent. of the general revenues is derived from the gross returns due to it.

These colonies have also a large estate in unalienated land, now yielding 17 per cent. of the general revenue, and as a matter of fact not more than 36 per cent. of the revenue is derived from taxation.

No satisfactory account of the loan expenditure of the National and Provincial Governments of the Argentine has yet been produced, and it is clear, from the statements laid before Congress by the National Government at present in power, that a very large proportion of this expenditure has been of a highly speculative and irregular character, the assets of uncertain value, and the direct returns exceedingly limited. It does not appear that the Provincial Governments are now possessed of any considerable quantity of land suitable for present occupation. Alienation seems to have taken place on an enormous scale, and it is not seen that receipts from land sales or rents figure amongst the revenue items of the Governments. It is therefore mainly on taxation that they must rely for the discharge of their obligations.

It seems probable that about 86 per cent. of the actual revenue is now raised by taxation, and this would represent in 1889 about £3. 0s. 4d. per head of the population, the total revenue in that year from all sources being £3. 10s. per head.

The taxation per head in Australia, colonial and local, amounts to £3. 18s. per head out of a total revenue of £8. 19s. per head.

Account must also be taken of the serious falling off in the Argentine National and Provincial revenues due to the large decrease in imports, and to the further depreciation of the paper currency which has taken place during 1890 and 1891.

There is reason to fear that the aggregate revenue (National, Provincial, and Municipal) for 1891 has not exceeded eight or nine millions sterling, or from £2 to £2. 5s. per head of the population.

In Australia in 1889 the aggregate expenses of administration by the several Colonial Governments, exclusive of the working expenses of the State railways, the interest on the public debt, and immigration, amounted to £3. 15s. 4d. per head of the population, and if we assume that this represents the cost of government conducted on an honest although very liberal scale, in a partially-developed and sparsely-populated country, it would seem that there can be no margin of revenue available in Argentine at present for meeting the interest on the foreign debt.

As a matter of fact, the annual receipts from customs have fallen by about two and a half millions sterling since 1889, while those from bank and railway shares have disappeared.

The condition of the Argentine Republic as respects the relative proportions of her debt and revenue, although unsatisfactory, is by no means unparalleled.

In the subjoined statement the revenue and debt of several of the Colonies, as well as various European nations, per head of the population, the percentage of the revenue represented by the interest of the debt, and the number of years' revenue, the sum of which would be equal to the debt in each case, are shown :—

COUNTRY.		Debt per head of the Population.			Revenue per head of Population.			Interest on Debt percentage of Total Revenue.	Debt Multiple of Revenue.
		£ s. d.			£ s. d.			Per cent.	Per cent.
ARGENTINE REPUBLIC,* 1880	...	27 0 0			3 10 0			49·5	77
Ditto 1891	...	30 0 0			3 0 0			98·1	110·0
Ditto 1880 (Cedulas and currency excluded)	...	16 0 0			3 10 0			85·1	45
Ditto 1891 Ditto	...	19 0 0			3 0 0			67·3	55
AUSTRALIA† 1890	...	45 14 8			8 19 4			51·6	12
NEW ZEALAND 1890	...	68 8 0			6 10 0			56·6	85
CANADA 1890	...	11 18 8			1 10 0			57·6	7·9
FRANCE 1890	...	30 3 8			3 16 10			58·8	104
PORTUGAL 1890	...	28 15 11			2 1 9			89·0	120
UNITED KINGDOM† 1890	...	28 10 0			3 12 0			58·6	8·5

* (Includes the Revenue of the Provinces and Municipalities as well as the National Revenue.)

† In these cases the figures include local Debt and Revenue.

D

In this table the circumstances of the Argentine
Republic are represented under four conditions. In
the first the revenue of 1889 is compared with a
debt which includes the liabilities more or less contingent on account of the note circulation and the
Cedula Bonds. In the second the same debt is compared with the revenue of 1891, estimated on the basis
of the Presidential statements. In the third and fourth
the debt, exclusive of the liabilities of a contingent
character above referred to, is compared with revenues
of 1889 and 1891 respectively. In all four cases, as well
as in other statements relating to the Argentine, the
figures representing revenue include that of all the
Provinces and Municipalities as well as the revenue of
the National Government.

When considering the relations between production
and debt in Australia and the Argentine respectively,
the conclusion cannot be avoided that, in order to make
a fair comparison between the capacities of the two
countries for meeting their liabilities, the expenditure
on railways by private companies in the latter should
be included in its debt.

In Australia the railway revenue is collected by the
Government, and forms a part of the general revenue of
the country. In the Argentine the railway revenue is
collected by the companies who own the lines, and
nearly the whole of the net profit is remitted to Europe.
It results in either case that interest on the cost of
construction is a tax levied on the inhabitants.

This is in fact admitted in the case of Australia,
since the amount representing her debt in the foregoing
statement includes the expenditure on railway construction. If a similar course be adopted with reference
to the Argentine, an addition of £15 must be made to

the several amounts representing in the same statement
the debt per head of the population.

Reverting to the statement given above, in which
the revenue per head of the population in various
countries is shown, it will be seen that the Argentine
revenue of 1889, and in an even greater degree that of
1891, is far below the standard of Australia and New
Zealand—countries in many respects similarly cir-
cumstanced. This is due, firstly, to the fact that the
expenditure of a very large proportion of the loans contracted by the Government has been non-productive of
revenue, although perhaps to some extent favouring
the production of commodities ; secondly, to the non-
development of the mining and mineral industries, and
the want of sufficient capital and energy for the proper
development of the pastoral resources of the country ;
and, thirdly, to the former wholesale alienation of the
Government lands, which has deprived the country of
an important source of revenue which the Australian
Colonies now enjoy.

The millions squandered may perhaps be pursued by
enhancing the taxes on land and immovable property,
and by levying others on incomes and the fortunes left
by deceased persons. Some of the benefits conferred by
the immense extension of railways, which has added
enormously to the value of real property, would thus be
appropriated by the State.

Notwithstanding the grave mistakes and malversa-
tions which have been connected with the past expenditure of the Government, and the burdens thereby laid
on the nation, there is much to justify a belief that if
political disturbances can be avoided and a fairly honest
Government maintained in power, the country will continue to increase very rapidly in wealth and population,

and that the present conditions of depression and collapse of credit represent but a passing phase.

The Provinces, which are now fairly opened up by railways, are for the most part fertile, the land is easily cultivated and cheap, access to the seaboard is easy, and the distance which separates the country from the markets of Europe not more than half that which has to be traversed by Australian produce. It would be indeed extraordinary if these advantages failed to attract both labour and capital.

For the European holder of Argentine securities the most important questions are—what would be the effect of any assumed increase in the population and wealth of the country on the capacity of the Government for meeting its obligations, and within what period is it probable that the increase in these two factors will be sufficiently large to enable the Government to place itself, by means of taxation, or by otherwise utilising the resources of the country, in a solvent position.

It would be difficult under any circumstances or with regard to any country to answer such questions with confidence, but in the case of the Argentine Republic the difficulty is increased tenfold by the doubt thrown on all the available statistics and statements by the duplicity which characterised the transactions and utterances of the Government which was displaced by the revolution of August, 1890.

There is much reason to regret that the present Government, which has inaugurated a policy of retrenchment and reform, has not yet seen its way to invite to the country and take into its confidence a Commission authorised to represent the European bondholders, not with a view to its interference in the slightest degree with the proceedings of the Government, but in order that it might investigate the financial situation on the spot with their assistance, make themselves acquainted with the resources of the country and its prospects, advise the Government when asked to do so with reference to measures under consideration affecting the interests of the bondholders, and report to the latter from time to time with reference to such measures and proposals, and as to the result of their inquiries into all the matters above referred to.

There can be little doubt that if such a course were pursued, it would greatly tend to the re-establishment of credit and general confidence, and would stimulate the inflow of capital, for the profitable investment and employment of which in the production of raw materials and food for export, and the purchase of unduly depreciated property, there has perhaps never existed better opportunity.

All the most reliable reports on the country tend to prove that there are many directions in which its resources could be exploited with every prospect of successful results. It has been incidentally mentioned that, as respects the production of wool per sheep and its average quality, the flocks of the Argentine are far inferior to those of Australia.

If brought up to the Australian standard (and there seems to be no reason why they should not be), the yearly clip would be at the least doubled in value, and this would imply an increase in exports of 8 millions sterling on that account alone.

Again it has been shown year after year that the arrangements for the transfer of wheat, maize, and other agricultural produce to the seaboard, and for shipping such produce, are extremely defective, and often entail heavy loss to producers and consignees. Much damage

is done by the exposure of the produce to the vicissi-
tudes of the weather. It has been asserted that not one
of the great railway companies possesses shipping facilities for cereals which are worthy of the name, those
which exist for the shipment of wool not being suitable
for grain. The agriculturist as a rule possesses neither
barns nor sheds, and carries his produce as soon as
possible to the nearest railway station, where it is often
stacked for weeks in the open air. All this reduces the
average margin of profit and checks cultivation.

The introduction of the system largely developed and
successfully worked in the United States for the purchase of cereals from the farmers at convenient local
centres on railways, or the issue to them of negotiable
warrants for grain delivered at such centres, and the
provision there of arrangements for cleaning, sampling,
grading, elevating, and storing grain in readiness for
transportation to the sea coast would benefit the pro-
ducer, the railway company, the shipper, the dealer,
and ultimately the consumer. The first would be early
relieved of all anxiety in regard to the fate of his har-
vested produce. The railway would be worked at a
more uniform pressure, and consequently more economi-
cally than is possible under existing circumstances,
seeing that it is overwhelmed at harvest time with
freight, for which it is called upon to provide rolling
stock and locomotive power, which again becomes
redundant at other seasons. The shipper and the dealer
would be saved in a great measure from the risk of loss
incidental to the receipt and delivery of produce which
is unsound, or in which a process of deterioration has
commenced, or which is of varied quality, and the consumer, on whom all losses are ultimately thrown, would
satisfy his requirements at less cost.

The railways have now been so far extended towards
the Andes that the question of the development of the
mineral resources of the country should receive the
serious attention of the Argentine Government.

The speculative character of all mining enterprises
and the uncertainty as to results, especially in the case
of vein mining, should be recognised, and a very liberal
policy should be adopted in regard to the terms on
which concessions are granted and taxes or royalties
are levied. Nevertheless the Government should dis-
tinguish between the capitalist acting in good faith in
the furtherance of legitimate exploitation, and that
curse of every country the promoter of bogus concerns,
and the vendor who bases his demands on the false
reports of so-called experts in mining hired for the
occasion.

Their hands should be free to endorse or refute
the reports which are intended to support appeals to
the public for money, and the valuations of concessions
for mining, appearing in the Argentine territory or in
Europe, and to require the publication of such official
statements in the newspapers issued in either country
or on the face of prospectuses under penalty of
forfeiture of concessions obtained.

Very considerable sums are yearly expended by the
Australian Governments in exploration and in mineral
and geological surveying. The work of exploration
includes deep boring with the diamond drill and other
appliances. It would be too much to expect of the
Argentine Government at the present time that they
should embark on any extensive work of that kind, but
looking to the immense importance to the country of a
cheap supply of fuel, it would be a wise step to
prosecute some search for a workable bed of coal.

Practically speaking the whole surface of the country is formed of sedimentary deposits, the result of the working down of the Andes, and the highlands of the central portion of the continent. These form a continuous covering concealing the underlying formations.

It seems to be eminently a case in which the use of the boring tool is indicated, as the sole means of acquiring a knowledge of the character and mineral resources of the latter.

The progress of the country in the immediate future obviously depends on a number of factors the individual weight of which there is little means of estimating. It is certain that if the expectation of profit to be obtained in the Argentine territory can be fairly aroused, nothing will prevent the inflow of labour and capital to secure that profit. But the expectation of profit may be destroyed by excessive taxation, by unwise legislation, or by civil war.

If the increase of population during the twenty years from 1869 to 1889 be taken as an index to the increase which may be expected in the future, the number of inhabitants in the Argentine at the end of five years, say in January, 1897, should amount to 5,600,000. If, moreover, the amount of taxation per head were maintained at the level of 1889, the ordinary revenue would at the date in question reach £20,000,000.

In this case, as in all others in which the ordinary revenue is referred to in this paper, the term includes the ordinary revenue of the Provinces and Municipalities as well as that of the National Government. With strict economy in administration it should be practicable to set aside £5,000,000 out of such revenue for the payment of interest on the foreign and internal debt.

In the foregoing estimate of the situation, no account

has been taken of possible increase of production due to better management, and the consequent capacity of the people to sustain a higher rate of taxation, or to the liquidation of a portion of the internal debt by the realisation of the assets of the Government banks of issue or the Mortgage banks.

It is deducible from the foregoing statement that it should be practicable for the country to commence at an earlier date than that mentioned the partial payment of interest on loans.

It may be contended that the commercial and financial crisis from the effects of which the country is suffering has so much depressed credit and enterprise that immigrants are no longer attracted, are not likely to be attracted for a very considerable time, and that consequently the foregoing estimate of the prospective increase of the population will not by any means be realised.

It must, however, be recollected that the people who have entered the country in such vast numbers within the past ten or fifteen years consist in the main of the industrious and thrifty peasants of Italy, Spain, and France, who have found in the cultivation of the cheaply-obtained and fertile land of the Republic a source of profit far greater than any available in the densely-populated areas of Southern Europe. The promise for the agricultural industry, now only in its infancy, was never greater than it is at present, and there is no climate in the Western hemisphere which is so well suited to the Latin race.

Neither pastoral nor agricultural products have diminished in volume in consequence of the severe crisis which has prevailed, and it can hardly be doubted that the tide of immigration will before long resume its flow,

and reach, at any rate, the dimensions assumed ; and
which are not, be it remembered, those of the more
remarkable and recent years, but the average of a long
period, at the commencement of which the movement
was comparatively small.

It is a remarkable circumstance and an evidence of
the docility, patience, and resourcefulness of the labour-
ing class of the country, that although thousands of
them engaged on various public works have been thrown
out of employment and have lost their savings which
were deposited in the defaulting National and State
Banks, there has been no rioting and no attacks on
property. There would have been demonstrations and
serious disturbances in most European countries under
similar circumstance, and in Australia demands for
relief works which the Government would be powerless
to resist.

The broad conclusions which the circumstances seem
to justify, so far as they can be read from the imperfect
details available to those who are not in the confidence
of the Argentine Government or their financial agents,
are that the situation although serious is not desperate,
that sacrifices on the part of the creditors of the Republic
are inevitable, but that they need not be of that crush-
ing character which some suppose, although they must
of course vary in extent with the nature of the security
held. And it may be as well to recollect, when terms of
composition are proposed, that it is not always the
interest of the compounding debtor to give the best
possible account of his means to the creditors whom he
may invite to confer with him.

It has happened, and it will doubtless happen again,
that the creditors of a defaulting foreign government
have been invited to meet its financial representatives,

or those of the houses which have floated the loans, in order to consider terms of composition.

A bald statement has been made with reference to the inability of the country to meet its liabilities, and representing that the terms offered are the only ones to be hoped for, and that their fulfilment will tax to the utmost the available resources of the Government.

The reflection which must naturally occur to those who hear such statements is, that if such an accurate analysis of the economic condition of the country can be made as to justify positive assertions such as those which have preceded the invitation to the creditors to make sacrifices of the most extreme character, the analysis should have taken place before the loans were contracted for which involved the country so deeply as to render it unable to meet its engagements.

The ordinary investor in the scrip of a loan delegates the task of previous investigation to the financial houses issuing the loan, and makes his investment in reliance on its character, acumen, and standing, and he must take the consequences if his reliance has been misplaced, but he can hardly be expected, when terms of composition have to be arranged, and investigation has again to be made, in order to settle the nature of the agreement, to lean altogether on the reed which has already pierced his hand. He may rightly require that all the facts on which a judgment has to be formed should be put clearly and in detail before him.

In the foregoing pages a very rude and imperfect outline has been given of some of the considerations which bear on the questions for settlement between the Argentine Government on the one hand and their creditors on the other. In the interval which remains during which payments on account of the service of the debt of the country have been suspended, under the arrangements suggested by Lord Rothschild's Committee, and adopted by the Argentine Government, there is opportunity, on the one hand, for the Government to take what measures they may for rehabilitating the finances of the country, and on the other for the preparation by competent hands of a correct and properly proportioned picture of the whole situation, which may form a point of departure for the thorough examination and discussion of any proposed arrangement by all concerned.

EFFINGHAM WILSON AND CO., PRINTERS, ROYAL EXCHANGE, E.C.